READING COMPREHENSION SERIES • LEVEL A

WAGS AND TAGS

Martha K. Resnick
Carolyn J. Hyatt
Sylvia E. Freiman

About the Authors

MARTHA K. RESNICK is an experienced elementary teacher, formerly a Reading Resource Teacher with the Baltimore City Schools. She has served as a cooperative practice teacher, training student teachers from many colleges. Mrs. Resnick received her master's degree in education at Loyola College.

CAROLYN J. HYATT has taught elementary, secondary, and adult education classes. She was formerly a Senior Teacher with the Baltimore City Schools. Mrs. Hyatt received her master's degree in education at Loyola College.

SYLVIA E. FREIMAN has taught primary and upper elementary grades. She has conducted teacher in-service classes, supervised student teachers, and participated in curriculum planning. Mrs. Freiman received her master's degree in education at Johns Hopkins University.

Reading Comprehension Series

Wags & Tags
Claws & Paws
Gills & Bills
Manes & Reins
Bones & Stones
Swells & Shells
Heights & Flights
Trails & Dales

Acknowledgments

Illustrated by Rosemarie Fox-Hicks

Cover design Linda Adkins Design

Cover photograph © Ron Kimball Photography

ISBN 0-8114-1339-X

Copyright © 1993 Steck-Vaughn Company

All rights reserved. No part of the material protected by this copyright may be reproduced or utilized in any form or by any means, electronic or mechanical, including photocopying, recording, or by any information storage and retrieval system, without permission in writing from the copyright owner. Requests for permission to make copies of any part of the work should be mailed to: Copyright Permissions, Steck-Vaughn Company, P.O. Box 26015, Austin, TX 78755.

Printed in the United States of America

12 13 PO 04 03 02 01 00

Contents

Story 1..4
A Vocabulary   B Sentence Comprehension

Story 2..7
A Sentence Comprehension   B Noting Details

Story 3..10
A Sentence Comprehension   B Noting Details

Story 4..13
A Vocabulary   B Sentence Comprehension

Skills Review (Stories 1–4)......16
A Noting Details   B Vocabulary

Story 5..18
A Drawing Conclusions   B Classifying

Story 6..21
A Question Comprehension   B Classifying
C Noting Details

Story 7..24
A & B Main Idea   C Drawing Conclusions

Story 8..27
A Noting Details   B Drawing Conclusions

Story 9..30
A Perceiving Relationships   B Vocabulary

Skills Review (Stories 5–9)......33
A Question Comprehension   B Main Idea
C Sentence Comprehension

Story 10..36
A Perceiving Relationships
B Drawing Conclusions

Story 11..39
A Main Idea & Facts   B Sentence Comprehension

Story 12..42
A Sentence Comprehension
B Question Comprehension

Story 13..45
A Classifying   B Vocabulary

Skills Review (Stories 10–13) ..48
A Vocabulary   B Main Idea   C Vocabulary

Story 14..51
A Drawing Conclusions   B Vocabulary
C Noting Details

Story 15..54
A Main Idea   B Vocabulary
C Sequencing   D Cause & Effect

Story 16..57
A Main Idea   B Perceiving Relationships
C Question Comprehension
D Predicting Outcomes

Skills Review (Stories 14–16) ..60
A Noting Details & Inferences
B & C Vocabulary   D Drawing Conclusions
E Main Idea   F Sequencing
G Noting Details & Question Comprehension

1

See the house.
People live in the house.
See the dogs.
See Wags. See Tags.

The people walk.
The people walk in the big house.
Wags walks in a little house.
Tags walks in a little house.

A Draw a circle around the right words.
One is done for you.

1.

dogs 

2.

Tags   house

3.

people   house

4.

big dog   little dog

5.

The dogs walk.

The people walk.

6.

a little house

a big house

B **Draw a line under the pictures that match each sentence.**

1. People live in houses.

a.
b.
c.
d.

2. The dogs walk.

a.
b.
c.
d.

The dogs see a new house.
The dogs see the new animal.
No! No! Not a cat!

A cat can not live here! No cat can live here!

See Tags run! See Wags run!
See the cat walk to the house.
Yes, a cat can live here!

A Write  yes or no .

One is done for you.

1. The dogs can see a new house. yes

2. A cat can live in a house.

3. A house is an animal.

4. Dogs can run.

5. A house can run.

6. The dogs see a new animal.

7. A house can walk.

B **Draw a circle around the sentence that matches the picture.**

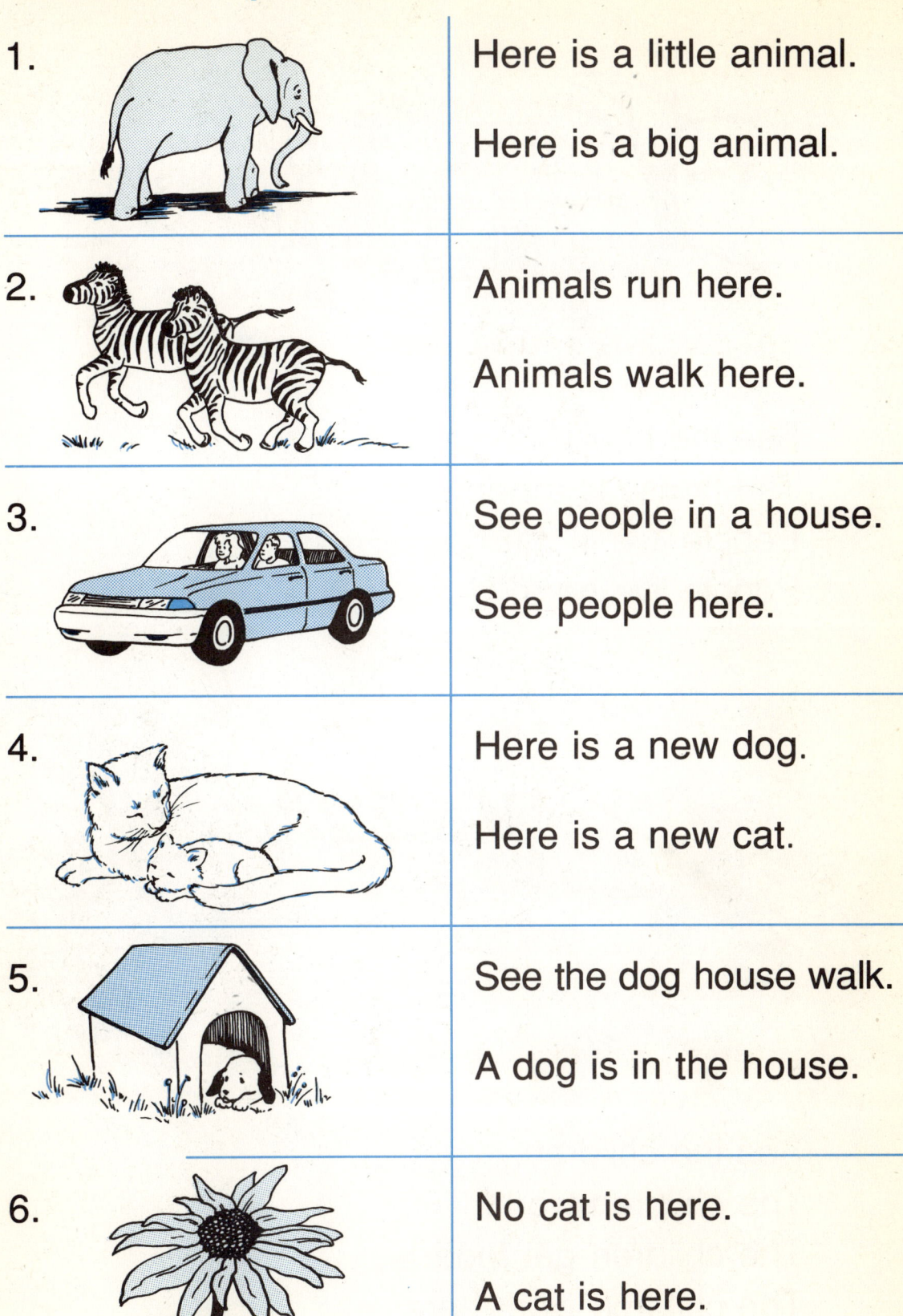

1. Here is a little animal.
   Here is a big animal.

2. Animals run here.
   Animals walk here.

3. See people in a house.
   See people here.

4. Here is a new dog.
   Here is a new cat.

5. See the dog house walk.
   A dog is in the house.

6. No cat is here.
   A cat is here.

9

3

See the house.
The house is a home.
People live in the house.
People live here.

See the children.
The children work.
The children get food.
The children work here.

A Draw a line under the ones who are working.

1.

2.

3.

4.

5.

6.

B Draw a circle around the sentence that matches the picture.

1.  Children get food.
Children live here.

2.  People live here.
Here is food.

3.  See a house.
Here is food.

4.  Children see food.
The house works.

5.  The people live here.
The people work here.

6.  People get food.
Here is a house.

4

Here is Dad.
Dad works here.
Dad works to get food.

See Mom.
Mom is working.
Mom works to get food.

See the children.
The children are here.
The children are working.

A **Write the best word to finish the sentence.**

1. Mom and Dad are ___.
   live   people

   people

2. Mom works to get ___.
   not   food

3. People ___.
   food   work

4. Children are in the ___.
   people   house

5. Here are the ___.
   homes   is

6. The people are ___.
   working   get

7. The children live ___.
   food   here

B Draw a circle around the picture that matches the sentence. One is done for you.

1. Here is Mom working.

   a.    b.

2. Dad and the children are here.

   a.    b.

3. The people get food.

   a.    b.

4. Children live here.

   a.    b.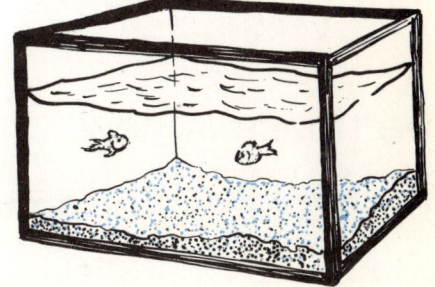

SKILLS REVIEW (Stories 1–4)

A Draw a circle around the right words.

1.

not new   new

2.

not new   new

3.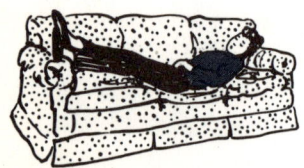

is working

is not working

4.

can not get food

can get food

5.

The house is new.

The house is not new.

6.

People live here.

People work here.

B **Write the best word to finish the sentence.**

1. See the children ____.
   not   walk

2. The people get a new ____.
   home   here

3. Can the children live ____?
   here   house

4. The house is ____.
   new   not

5. Dad and Mom get ____.
   new   food

6. The children are ____.
   working   can

7. Dad and Mom are ____.
   house   people

5

Here is a spider.
The spider can work.
The spider can make a new house.

See the new home.
The spider says,
"Walk in here, bugs.
Walk in the new house."

The spider can get food.
The spider eats a bug.

A **Read each question. Write yes or no.**

1. Can a house walk?　　　no

2. Can a spider eat bugs?

3. Can people walk?

4. Can children eat?

5. Can a house work for food?

6. Can a spider make a new home?

7. Can a spider walk?

B Read the words. Match the picture to the right word. One is done for you.

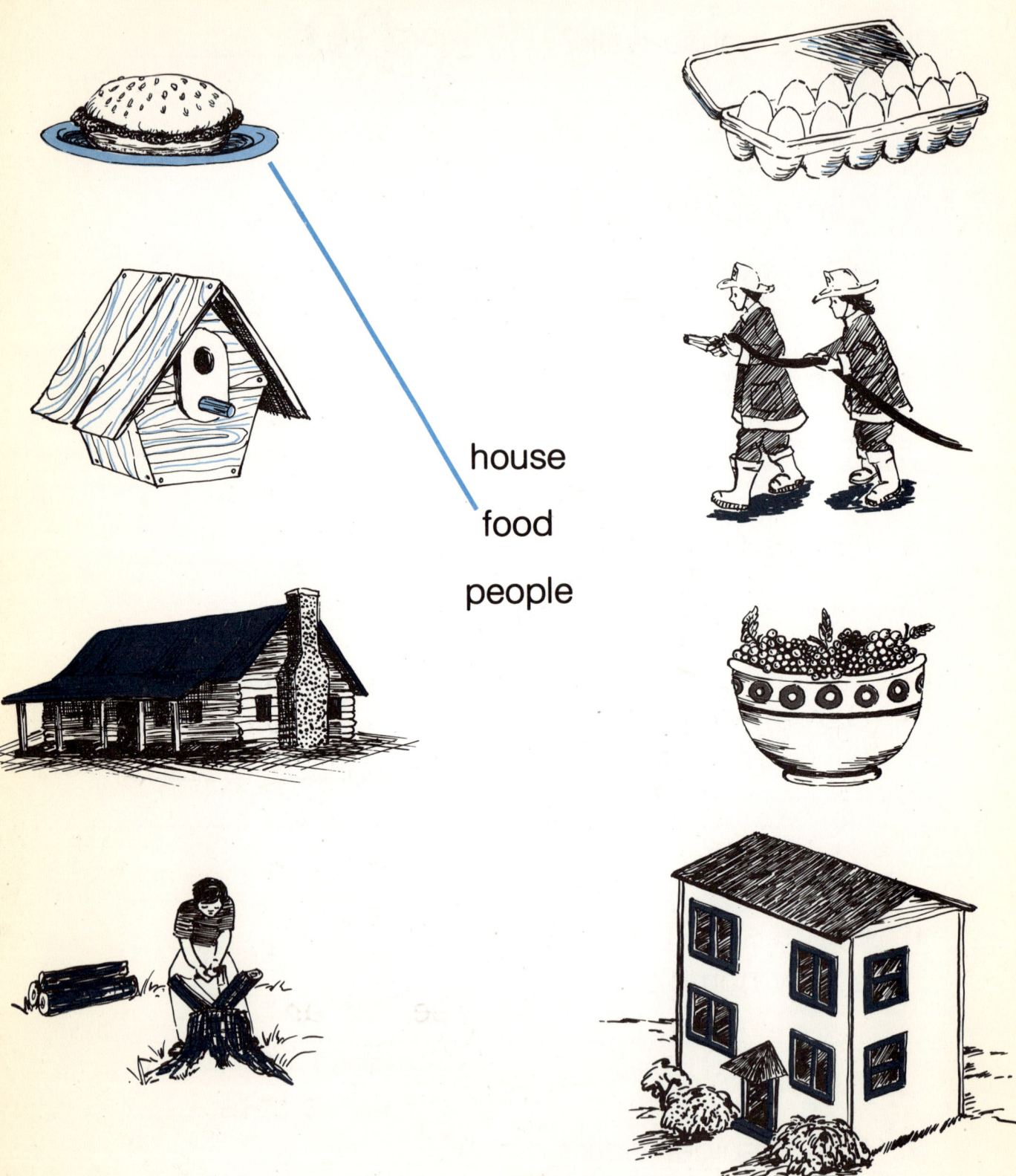

house

food

people

20

See Jill and Mom.
Mom works.
Here is what Mom can do.

See Will and Mom.
Mom can work.
See what Mom can do.

Here are Nan and Dad.
See Dad work.
Dad works and works.

See Dan and Dad.
Dad is working.
Dad works here.

21

A Who?
What? **Draw a line under the right one.**

1. Who can make a house?

2. What can not walk?

3. Who can eat?

   home   dad   live

4. What lives here?

   says   see   spider

5. Who can walk?

   food   mom   new

6. Who are people?

   a house   children and dad   walk and walk

7. Who can get a new house?

   mom and dad   live and eat   food and work

8. What can not eat?

   house   children   people

B Read the words. Put an X on the people.

Dan	Will	houses	not
walk	Mom	live	Dad
for	home	Nan	is
children	eat	food	get
do	new	Jill	in

C Draw a circle around the right words.

1.

can not walk

can eat

2.

can make food

are in a house

3.

works in a house

can eat

4.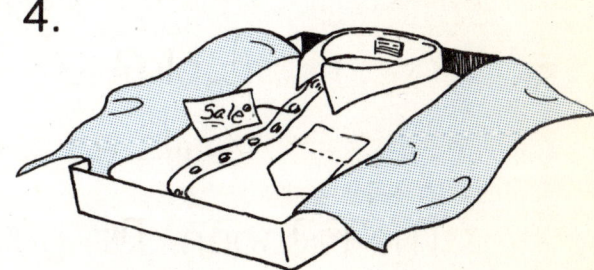

is not new

is new

7

See the tree.
The tree is a home.
What can live in the house?

See what lives here.
It is for a raccoon.
Raccoons can live in trees.

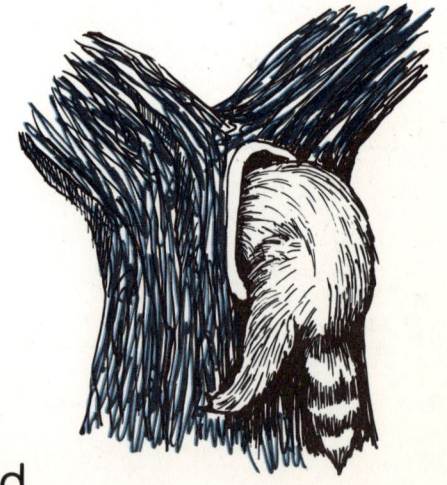

The raccoon can go in.
It can go out to get food.
It gets corn and fish to eat.

A Draw a line under the best name for this story.

   1. A House for a Fish
   2. The Raccoon's Home
   3. The Tree's Food

B Read each story. Draw a line under the best name for the story.

Will gets a fish to eat.
The raccoon sees Will.
It walks to Will.
Will says, "No, Raccoon!
The fish is for people."

1. The Raccoon Gets Food
   Will Eats the Raccoon
   Food for People

Dad Raccoon says, "Walk in!
Here is corn.
Eat and eat.
No people are here."

2. The People Eat Food
   The Raccoons Get Food
   The Raccoons Get Fish

C Read each sentence. Write yes or no.

1. A tree can have fish in it.

2. Raccoons can get a new home.

3. Corn is food for raccoons.

4. Jill can eat corn and fish.

5. Trees can eat raccoons.

6. A fish can eat.

7. Corn can walk out to a tree.

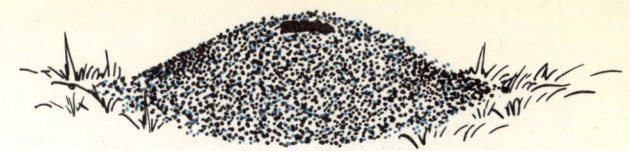

8 Can you see a house here?
Yes, the hill is a home.

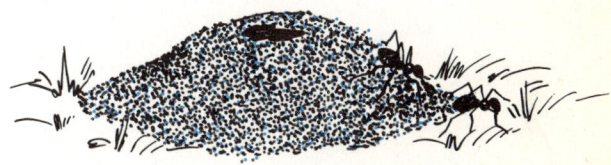

It is a home for bugs.
The little bugs are ants.
Many ants live in the house.
Many ants work in the hill.

Ants walk in and out.
They go out to get food.
They take food into the hill.

A **What do you see? Draw a circle around the right ones. There are 2 right ones for each picture.**

1. See a raccoon walk.
2. They eat corn.
3. They eat fish.
4. Here are 2 raccoons.

1. Many ants are working.
2. Many ants are in the house.
3. Many ants are walking.
4. The ants are eating corn.

1. I see children here.
2. Children eat fish.
3. Here are many fish.
4. Here are many children.

1. Children take corn.
2. They eat ants.
3. A raccoon takes a fish.
4. The raccoon will eat fish.

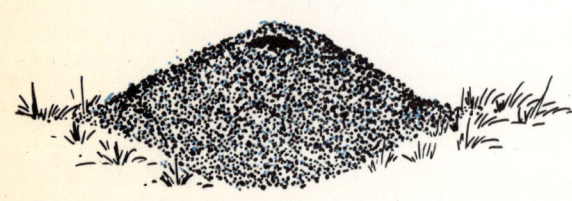

1. Raccoons live here.
2. Ants eat raccoons.
3. Ants live here.
4. Ants work here.

B Read each question. Write yes or no.

1. Do hills eat corn?

2. Are ants little?

3. Do many ants live in hills?

4. Do spiders live in little hills?

5. Do trees walk to ants?

6. Do many people work to get food?

7. Do trees eat raccoons?

9

What lives here?
Can children live here? No.
It is a home for bees.
Many bees live here.

Many bees work here.
They go to the flowers.
They take something from the flowers.

Bees take something into the house.
They make food from it.
The food is good to eat.
People will eat what the bees make.
What food do bees make?

A Can they get home? Draw a line to the right home.

1.

2.

3.

4.

5.

B Write the best word to finish the sentence.

1. Bees go to the ____.
   from   flowers

2. From flowers bees get ____.
   something   see

3. Bees take something ____.
   home   have

4. Bees make ____.
   flowers   food

5. The food is ____.
   go   good

6. People will eat ____.
   it   is

7. Corn is something to ____.
   it   eat

SKILLS REVIEW (Stories 5–9)

A **Who? What?** **Draw a line under the right one.**

1. Who can take a walk?

  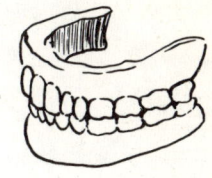

2. What can make something?

 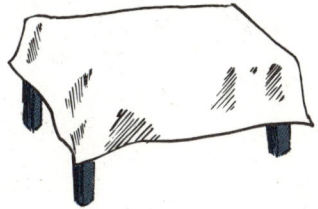 

3. What can not eat?

   raccoons   hills   bees

4. What can people do?

   make a new ant

   make a new house

   make a new raccoon

5. Who are **not** people?

   Nan and Dan

   bugs and flowers

   many children

33

B **Read each story. Draw a circle around a good name for it.**

Raccoons eat corn and fish.
Ants eat many foods.
Fish eat bugs.

1. Who Can Walk?
2. What Animals Eat
3. What Bugs Eat

The children take a walk.
They go to the flowers.
They get many flowers.
They take the flowers to Mom.

1. The Flowers Walk
2. Mom Takes a Walk
3. Something for Mom

C **What do you see? Draw a circle around the right ones. There are 2 right ones for each picture.**

1. Raccoons live in the flowers.
2. Bees take something from flowers.
3. Bees work here.
4. The bees make a home.

1. Dan gets something new.
2. Dan gets something to eat.
3. Dan sees something new here.
4. Dan takes a walk.

10

The tree is a home.
It is a house.
See what lives here.

Here is the squirrel's home.
One squirrel lives here.
The squirrel climbs the tree.

Two birds live here.
They fly home.

What lives here?
Bugs live here.
Little bugs climb the tree.

A What is at home here? Write the words in the correct spaces. Use these words.

squirrel   raccoon   children   bird   people

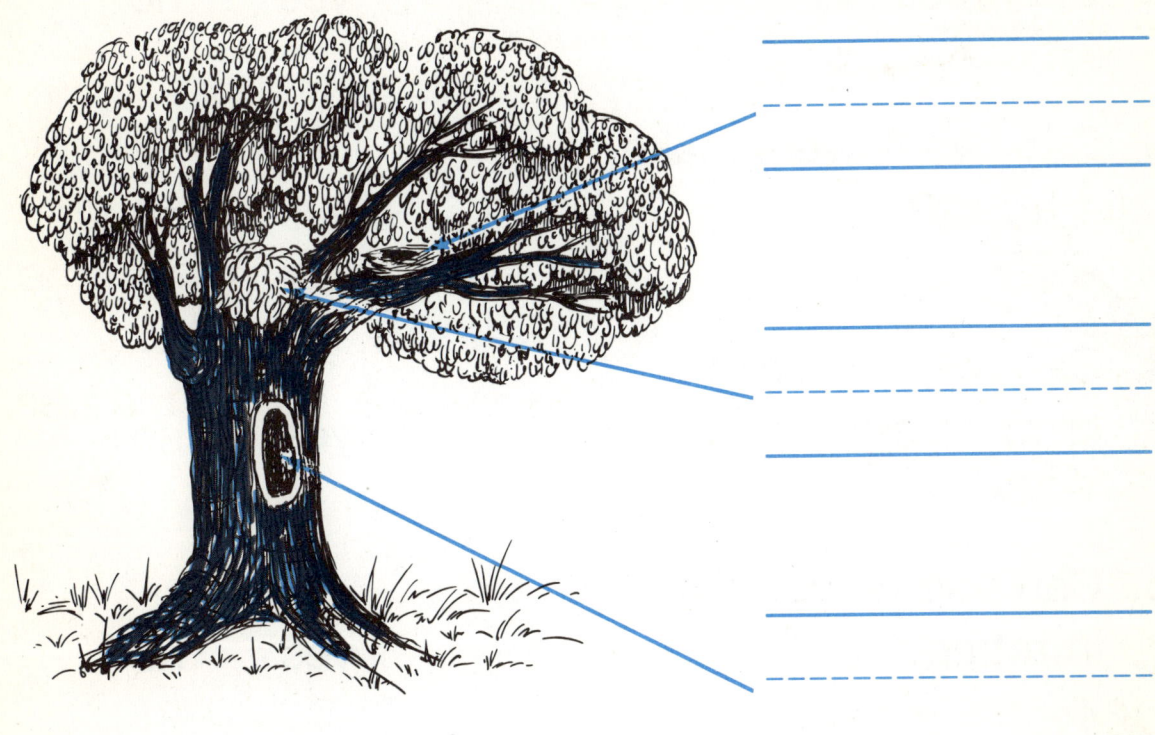

B **Read each question. Circle yes or no.**

1. Can a squirrel climb?　　　　　　　　yes　　no

2. Can trees fly?　　　　　　　　　　　　yes　　no

3. Can two flowers make
   a house?　　　　　　　　　　　　　　yes　　no

4. Can two little children
   climb trees?　　　　　　　　　　　　yes　　no

5. Can one raccoon live
   in a tree?　　　　　　　　　　　　　yes　　no

6. Can one squirrel take a walk?　　　　yes　　no

7. Can fish live in hills?　　　　　　　　yes　　no

8. Do bugs climb?　　　　　　　　　　　yes　　no

9. Do hills fly?　　　　　　　　　　　　yes　　no

10. Is corn something good
    to eat?　　　　　　　　　　　　　　yes　　no

11

Here is a pond.
What can be in a pond?
Many animals can live here.

Ducks live here.
The ducks look for food.
They look in the water.

See the duck!
Look at its food.
Fish live in water.
Little fish can be food for ducks.

What can be in the pond?

bugs   frogs   flowers

39

A Which one is right? Put a ✔ by it.
One is done for you.

1. What is a good name for this story?

   _____ a. Water in the House

   _____ b. People in the Pond

   ✔ c. Animals in the Pond

2. What is **not** in this story?

   _____ a. a duck eating

   _____ b. what a bug eats

   _____ c. water in a pond

3. What animals can live in water?

   _____ a. people

   _____ b. frogs

   _____ c. squirrels

4. What do ducks do in the water?

   _____ a. climb trees

   _____ b. take a walk

   _____ c. look for food

5. What can eat fish?

   _____ a. people, raccoons, and ducks

   _____ b. ducks, ponds, and trees

   _____ c. flowers, trees, and houses

B Look at the pictures. Read the sentences.
Match each picture to the best sentence.

a.

1. The frog is not in the pond.

2. Two people play in the water.

b.

3. It looks for something to eat.

c.

4. The fish eats the flower.

d.

5. The bug can fly.

12

Many animals live in ponds.
They have to swim.
See the grass by the pond.
Animals can live in the grass.

Frogs live in the pond.
They go into the grass, too.

Ducks can be in the grass.
They can go into the water, too.

Many animals play in the water.
Many animals play by the water.
They have fun.

A Read each sentence. Draw a line under the correct picture. One is done for you.

1. Mom can swim.
   a.    b.

2. I have fun.
   a.    b.

3. Children play by a tree.
   a.    b.

4. Bees fly home.
   a.    b.

5. Fish can live here.
   a.    b.

B **Who?**
What? **Draw a circle around the right one.**

1. Who lives in a hill?
   are   ant   out

2. Who will eat corn?
   be   by   bird

3. What is something to eat?
   can   corn   climb

4. Who can live in water?
   dad   duck   do

5. Who gets something from flowers?
   bee   be   by

6. Who can have fun?
   play   pond   people

7. Who can have a home?
   are   ant   out

13

The bug says, "Look! I am big."
The bird says, "No! I am big.
You are little."

The bird says, "I am little."
The fox says, "Yes, you are little.
I am big."

Dad says, "Look here, Fox.
I am big.
You are the little one."
The fox says, "I can look.
I can see you.
You are the big one."

A Draw a line from each sentence to the correct picture. One is done for you.

a.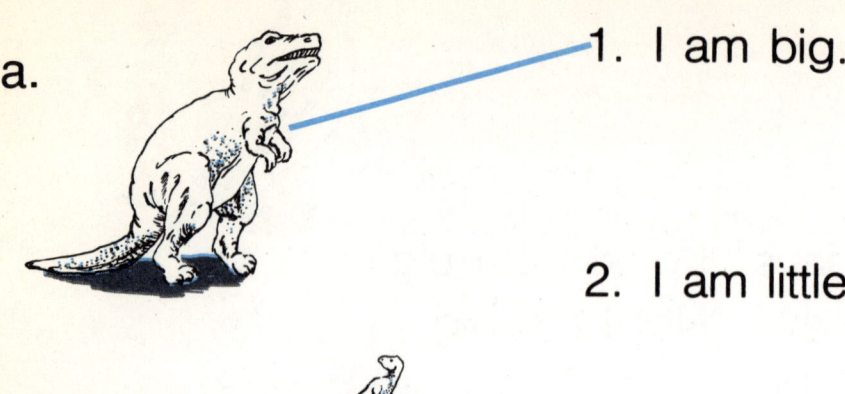

1. I am big.

2. I am little.

b.

---

a.

3. It is something little.

4. It is something big.

b.

---

a.

5. See the little one.

6. See the big one.

b.

B **Write the best word to finish the sentence.**

1. The bird looks for food.

    It will eat _____.
        children   bugs

2. Here is something good to eat.

    People will eat _____.
        fish   fly

3. A fox will climb.

    It can climb a _____.
        hill   pond

4. Animals can have fun.

    They will _____.
        play   pond

5. The frogs have fun in the water.

    They will _____.
        swim   fly

SKILLS REVIEW (Stories 10–13)

A **Write the name of each thing in the picture. Use these words.**

grass   fish   duck
raccoon   flower   frog

B **Read each story. Draw a circle around a good name for it.**

The fox and the frog play.
They play by the water.
They play in the grass.
They have fun.

1. The Fox Eats
2. The Animals Have Food
3. The Animals Have Fun

The fox says, "I will get something good to eat."
The frog says, "You will not get a frog to eat."
The frog gets into the water.
A little frog can swim.
A fox can not swim.

1. The Fox Will Not Eat a Frog
2. The Fox Eats a Frog
3. The Fox Gets a Duck

C **Write the best word to finish the sentence.**

1. Mom will go out to play.

   Mom will have _____.
             fly   fun

2. Jill has something to eat.

   Jill has _____.
       corn   climb

3. The flower is little.

   A flower can not _____.
         something   swim

4. The spider has a new home.

   The spider will get many _____.
           hills   bugs

5. Dad has something new.

   Dad says, "It is for _____."
         you   out

14

Chipmunk says, "I have a good house.
It is in the ground by the rocks."
A big fox says, "I want to see where
Chipmunk lives."

Chipmunk runs home.
The home is in the ground.

The fox says, "I see where Chipmunk lives.
I want to eat.
I will get into Chipmunk's house."
The fox is not happy.
She says, "I am too big.
I can not get into the little home."

A **Make a circle around the best ending for each sentence.**

1. The fox wants to get into the chipmunk's house. She wants to

    a. play with the chipmunk.

    b. swim with the chipmunk.

    c. get food.

2. The fox can not get into the chipmunk's home. The fox says,

    a. "I will not eat a duck."

    b. "I will not eat a chipmunk."

    c. "I will eat good rocks."

B **Write the word to finish the sentence. Use these words.**

| fox | lives | run | ground |

1. A chipmunk's house is in the _____.

2. The chipmunk can _____.

3. Here is where the animal _____.

C Underline the words that match the picture.

1.

not on the ground
on the ground

2.

happy people
happy ducks

3.

the rock
two rocks

4.

a frog by a bug
a frog by a flower

5.

on the grass
on the water

6.

is a bird
is not a bird

15

Chipmunk says, "I am happy.
The fox can not get me."

Here comes a snake.
She says, "I am not too big.
I will get into Chipmunk's house.
I like to eat little animals."
Chipmunk sees the snake.
She runs back into her house fast.

The snake is fast too.
She is in Chipmunk's house.

Chipmunk says, "The snake can not get me.
I have a back door to my house!
The back door is by the rocks."

A Underline the best name for the story.

1. Food for a Chipmunk
2. A Snake in the House
3. Food for a Fox

B Write the word to finish the sentence. Use these words.

| fast | me | rocks | door |

1. A chipmunk runs _____.

2. She runs out the _____.

3. The back door is by the _____.

C What came first in the story? Write **1** in the box next to it. What came next? Write **2**. What came last? Write **3**.

☐ Chipmunk runs out the back door.

☐ Chipmunk runs into the house.

☐ Snake gets into Chipmunk's house.

55

D **What will come next? Put a ✔ by it. One is done for you.**

1. The snakes have no food.

   ____ a. So they are happy.

   ✔ b. So they look for something to eat.

   ____ c. So they go to live with a spider.

2. The frogs are in the pond.

   ____ a. So they will run.

   ____ b. So they will walk.

   ____ c. So they will swim.

3. The bugs have a home in the tree.

   ____ a. So they have to climb.

   ____ b. So they have to swim.

   ____ c. So they can get a fish.

4. The spider works to make a new house.

   ____ a. So she will get bugs to eat.

   ____ b. So she will get a bird.

   ____ c. So she will live in the ant hill.

5. The snake gets into Chipmunk's house.

   ____ a. So the snake works with Chipmunk.

   ____ b. So the chipmunk and snake play.

   ____ c. So the chipmunk runs out the back door.

16

The duck says, "It is cold.
You will not see me, dogs.
I will go away. Good-by."

Tags says, "Where will you go?"
The duck says, "Where it is not cold."

The frog says, "Good-by, Tags.
Good-by, Wags.
I will go away too.
It is too cold."

Wags says, "Where will you go, frog?"

Frog says, "I go under the water here.
I get into the mud.
I will sleep in the mud."

Wags and Tags see the duck fly away.
They see the frog swim away.

Wags and Tags say, "It is cold.
We will go into the people's house."

A Draw a circle around the answer to each question.

1. What is this story about?
   a. Dogs sleep under the water.
   b. A cat is under the flowers.
   c. Animals want to go away.
2. What is not in the story?
   a. Wags says, "It is cold."
   b. A cat sleeps in the mud.
   c. A duck can fly away.

B Where is the bird? Draw a line from the words to the correct picture.

1.

under a flower

2.

on the corn

on a squirrel

4.

on the hill

5.

on a raccoon

6.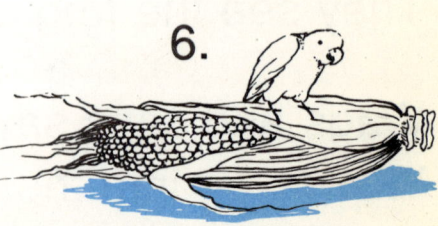

in a spider's home

C **Make a circle around the answer to each question.**

1. What can not fly away?

2. What do raccoons eat?

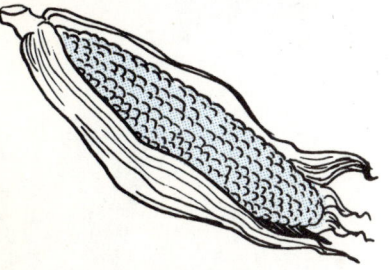  

3. Where is something under a tree?

4. What can you climb?

D **Will Wags and Tags ever see their friends again? Explain why.**

SKILLS REVIEW (Stories 14–16)

A <u>**Underline**</u> **the sentence that answers the question. One is done for you.**

1. What makes Dan happy?
   a. He has new flowers.
   b. <u>He has a new animal.</u>

2. Where is the bird?
   a. It plays by the tree.
   b. It is in its home.

3. Where is the bee?
   a. It is under the flower.
   b. It is on the flower.

4. Who can sleep?
   a. A door can sleep.
   b. A dog can sleep.

B **Write the best word to answer the question.**

1. Where do frogs sleep?

   mom   mud   many

2. Where can ducks fly?

   away   and   are

3. Who can come out the back door?

   rocks   flowers   people

4. What can go fast?

   a rock   a snake   ground

5. What can not be happy?

   a door   birds   children

6. Where do ants want to live?

   a door   a hill   a pond

7. What do spiders want to eat?

   people   rocks   bugs

C **Write the word to finish the sentence. Use the words in the box.**

| ground   want   happy   fast |

1. People have fun. They are _____.

2. She can run _____.

3. What do you _____?

D **Underline the best answer.**

1. The bird wants to eat ants.

   a. So the ants have to run fast.

   b. So the ants play with the bird.

   c. So the ants eat the bird.

2. We like to fish.

   a. So we fly into the tree.

   b. So we live by the water.

   c. So we look for fish in the ground.

E Read the story. **Underline** the best name for the story.

The children want something to eat.
They get food they like.
They play and run fast.
They have fun.

1. The Happy People
2. The Happy Rocks
3. By the Door

F Read the story. What came first? Write **1** in the box next to it.
What came next? Write **2**.
What came last? Write **3**.

Dan says, "I do not want a big rock here.
I will take it out."
He gets the rock out.
Dan sees a big snake on the ground.

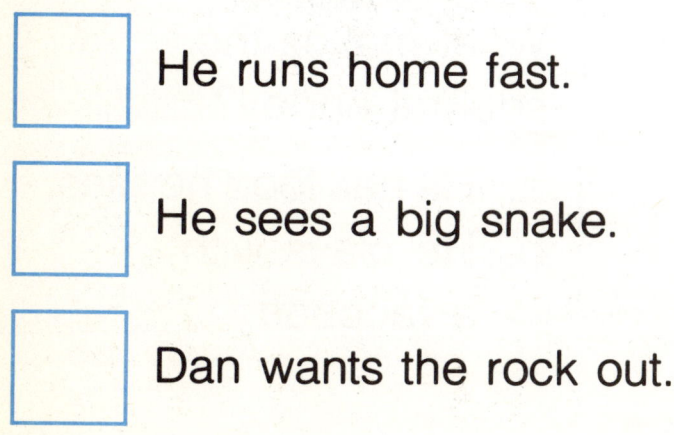

☐ He runs home fast.

☐ He sees a big snake.

☐ Dan wants the rock out.

G **Underline the sentence that answers the question.**

1.

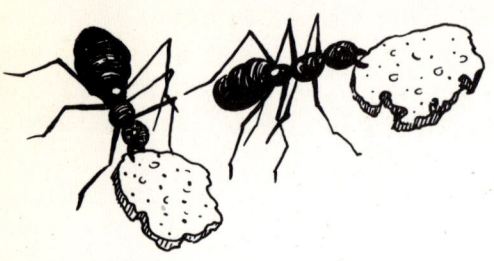

What do the ants do?

a. They play.

b. They work.

2.

What will the frog do?

a. She will walk on the ground.

b. She will swim.

3.

Where is the fish?

a. It is in the water.

b. It is by the water.

4.

What makes the squirrel happy?

a. He has food he likes.

b. He plays with a raccoon.